TOTALLY TALENTED PETS

by Cecile Skies
illustrated by Jim Talbot

SCHOLASTIC INC.

New York   Toronto   London   Auckland   Sydney
Mexico City   New Delhi   Hong Kong   Buenos Aires

ISBN-13: 978-0-439-89752-5
ISBN-10: 0-439-89752-1

12 11 10 9 8 7 6 5   7 8 9 10 11/0

Printed in the U.S.A.
First printing, February 2007

Welcome to the show! Like people, pets have lots of talents. There are as many talents as there are stars in the sky. Check out these totally talented pets!

This juggler is quick with her hands. Watch the balls fly through the air. Can she catch them all?

It sure helps to have some extra arms!

Are you ready to rock 'n' roll? These
friends love to play music together in a band.

Some songs are fast and some are slow.
It's best when they play a song everyone
knows. Then the crowd can sing along!

Watch as these trapeze artists swing from bar to bar. They do amazing twists and flips, and they make a great team.

Skateboarders move like lightning. They can do awesome jumps and crazy tricks.

Roller skaters are fast, too. Check out that perfect figure eight!

These friends are having so much fun, they
could jump all day! All they need is a rope and
some major energy!

Magicians can do almost anything.
They can even pull a carrot from a hat!

Some can even make themselves disappear.
Blending in is an extra-special trick.

Rah! Rah! Sis, boom, bah! Cheerleaders really have spirit. When they sing and clap, they make the crowd go wild.

They wave their fluffy pom-poms high in the air, and their skirts twirl around.

Bounce your head to the funky beat,
and watch the dancer move his feet.

He grooves and moves in perfect time
while a hip-hop rapper lays a rhyme.

Tightrope walking can be tricky. The long bar helps her balance. She's careful not to look down!

This is a talent that's made for the stage. Watch the dishes spin around as they balance on the sticks!

Unicycles are the trickiest kind of bike. With only one wheel, balance is key. It may not be easy, but it sure is fun.

This hula hooper is in the swing of things.
Watch as she moves her hips around and
around. She's really in the groove!

This stilt walker is up so high, her head is almost in the sky. The view is great from way up there, but it can get wobbly!

When a clown comes around, get ready to giggle. Clowns can make anything into something silly. Which is funniest—his nose, his shoes, or his big, colorful hair?

This gymnast's talent is doing outrageous backflips. Watch out!

Boing! Boing! Being on a pogo stick is bouncy.
It takes balance and strength to jump so high.

Yo-yos spin up, down, and around and around. Watch the yo-yo swing way into the air and then back down. What a cool trick!

Ready, set, blow! It's fun to make balloon animal shapes!

This ballet dancer is graceful and strong.
She dances smoothly and softly, and she looks
beautiful all in pink.

Some dances are loud and quick—like tap.
Clickity-click-clack! Tap dancers make a lot of noise!

Every pet has a talent, and every talent is different. That's what makes us unique. We hope you enjoyed the show!